what is your name in hebrew?

_____

Now *YOU* can read Hebrew!

שָׂרָה

דָּוִד

בִּנְיָמִין

רָחֵל

vowels are symbols that move around the letters

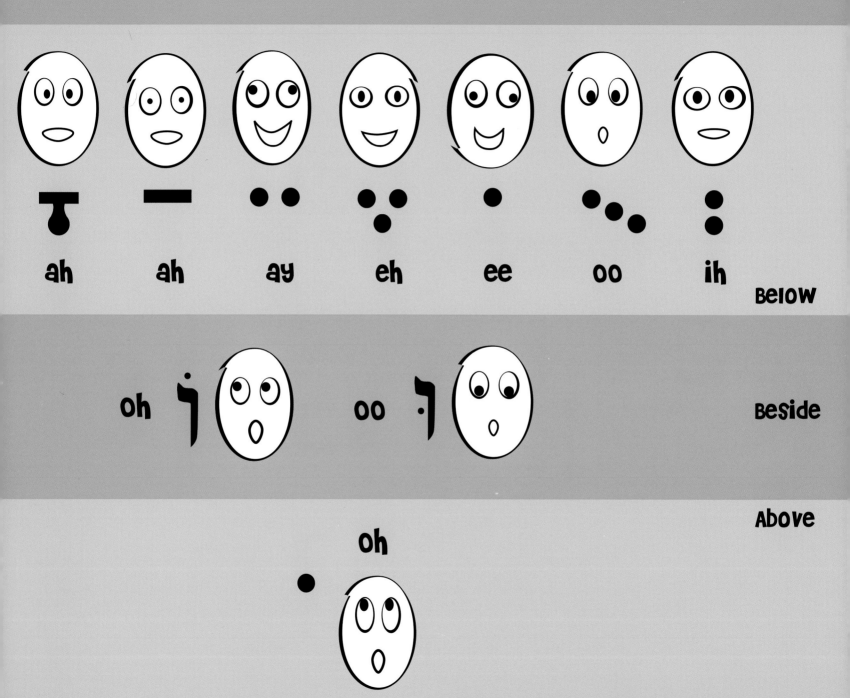

ah   ah   ay   eh   ee   oo   ih

Below

oh   oo

Beside

Above

oh

What are the Vowel Sounds and Symbols?

We have many of the same vowel sounds in Hebrew and in English. In Hebrew, the vowels are symbols that come below, beside or above the letters. Now that you are reading in Hebrew, REMEMBER, we read from right to left.

What do Sarah and David remember about the Aleph Bet that *YOU* should remember too!

There are 22 letters in the Aleph Bet. Each one is special.

What should you look for?
* ✳ corners and curves
* ✳ openings or closings
* ✳ letters on the line or dropping below it
* ✳ dots
* ✳ arms, legs, toes or tails

There are seven letter families. The letters in each family look and sound similar, but each letter has something special.

Five of the letter families include sofeet letters , final letters that only come at the end of a word. Except for Mem Sofeet, all the sofeet letters extend below the line. Look at the chart. Can you find them?

These are the letter families in order.

1. Bet	Vet	
2. Caf	Chaf	Chaf Sofeet
3. Mem		Mem Sofeet
4. Nun		Nun Sofeet
5. Pay	Fay	Fay Sofeet
6. Tzadi		Tzadi Sofeet
7. Shin	Sin	

TAV

Sarah:

Oh I love polish on my toe nails! Pink is my favorite. But why does the Tav have polish on its toes?

Lily:

Because Tav has toes!

What makes Tav special?

Shape: Tav has two legs that connect to its top. Tav sits on the line, and Tav has toes.

Sound: Tav's toes twinkle with toe polish. Tav "t" sound.

SHIN SIN

David:

Looks like Ben is sooooo cold and Rachel is sooooo hot.

Lily:

Right on. Ben is shivering. It's snowing on Ben and the letter Shin. Rachel is steaming hot. Rachel and the letter Sin are sizzling in the sun. Can you see that shin looks a lot like Sin. They're a family.

What makes Shin special?

Shape: Shin sits on the line and has three arms up in the air. Shin has a dot on the right. That dot puts the "sh" in Shin.

Sound: Ben SHivers in the SHnow. Shin "sh" sound.

What makes Sin special?

Shape: Sin also sits on the line and has three arms up in the air, but Sin has a dot on the left. The dot on the left puts the "sizzle" in the Sin.

Sound: Rachel Sizzles in the Sun. Sin "s" sound.

RESH

Sarah:

Look, Resh is round like a rollercoaster. I love rollercoasters!

Lily:

Exactly, Resh is round like a rollercoaster. Roarrrrrrr as you ride the rollercoaster.

ר

What's special about Resh?

Shape: Resh is round and lands on the line.

Sound: Resh is round like a rollercoaster. Resh "r" sound.

KOOF

Sarah:

Does that monkey have two tails or am I seeing things?

Lily:

Yes, you're right, that monkey has two tails. Those two tails actually look a lot like the letter Koof.

And in Hebrew, the word for monkey is Kof…which almost sounds like Koof.

What makes Koof special?

Shape: Koof has two parts. It has a curved top that sits on the line and one long leg that extends below the line.

Sound: So the kooky kids love their kooky kof with two tails that looks like the letter Koof. Koof "k" sound.

mrs. TZ   mr. TZ

TZADI
TZADI SOFEET

David:

Introducing Mr. and Mrs. Tuz?

Lily:

Almost. Introducing Mr. and Mrs. "TZ." You combine the T and the Z into one sound like the 'tz' sound inside the word pre'tz'el. That's how you make the "tz" sound of the letter Tzadi. Can you twist your arms like a pretzel to make the short arms of the Tzadi?

What makes Tzadi special?

צ ץ

Shape: Mr. Tz is the letter Tzadi. He's a cool dude sporting a big nose that points to the right.

Sofeet: Mrs. Tz is the letter Tzadi Sofeet , a final letter. She is a classy looking lady. Some say she looks like a tree with two branches…or shall we say "brantzes!" Tzadi Sofeet has one long leg that extends below the line.

Sound: Mr. Tz and Mrs. Tz are a cool looking family. Tzadi and Tzadi Sofeet "tz" sound.

FOREVER = FAY + PERGIE

PAY FAY
FAY SOFEET

Sarah:

Pergie and Fay, Forever? That sounds funny. I've only heard best friends forever.

Lily:

Well, Pergie and Fay are best friends. Pergie loves Fay, and they want to be together Forever.

What makes these lovebirds special? פ כ ף

Shape: Pergie is the letter Pay. Pay is rolled up like a curl and sits on the line. Pergie is having a bad skin day. Pergie has a pimple! Fay is the letter Fay. She's rolled up like a curl and also sits on the line. Fay is a beauty and doesn't have a pimple.

Sofeet: Forever is the letter Fay Sofeet,  another final letter. It curls at the top but has a long leg that extends below the line.

Sound: Pergie and Fay, Forever. Pay, Fay, Fay Sofeet "p" "f" "f" sound ♥ ♥ ♥

IYIN

David:

Look, Sarah and Rachel are hula dancing!

Lily:

Actually, let's say they're 'ula dancing!

What makes Iyin special?

Shape: Iyin has two long arms up in the air like Sarah and Rachel.

Sound: Iyin is special because it takes on the sound of the vowel it comes with.

Can you hear the "oo" in 'ula dancing?   "Ula, Ula, Ula" Iyin.

SAMECH

David:

Is that Ben and Rachel posing as Adam and Eve?

Lily:

Yes, that's Ben and Rachel in the Garden of Eden. And look, that Samech looks like the snake!

What makes Samech special?

Shape: Samech is round all over. It's curved and closed like a circle.

Sound: Samech is like a snake, and snakes hissssssssssssssssssssssssss . . . I'm outta here! Samech "s" sound.

NoBody   NoOne

NUN   NUN SOFEET

Sarah:

Who are NoOne and NoBody? That can't be their names. It sounds so lonely!

Lily:

Well, NoOne and NoBody are a pretty lonely family. NoOne is the letter Nun. He cries all the time. NoBody is the letter Nun Sofeet. NoBody is soooo long and soooo skinny that people don't notice her.

What makes Nun and Nun Sofeet special?

Shape: Nun has a short top and bottom and sits on the line.

Sofeet: Nun Sofeet is at the end of a word, a final letter. It has the same short top but a long leg that extends below the line.

Sound: People never remember NoOne and NoBody. Nun, Nun Sofeet "n" sound.

Do the loneliest couple in town a favor…don't forget them!!!

MORT

MOLLY

MEM   MEM SOFEET

David:

Molly and Mort! Are they a family too?

Lily:

Yes, they're a family. Molly is the letter Mem. Mort is the letter Mem Sofeet .

David:

And why is Molly losing her marbles?

Lily:

Well, that's what makes Molly, I mean Mem, special!

What makes Mem and Mem Sofeet special?

מ ם

Shape: Mem sits on the line, but is always open on the bottom. So poor Molly is always losing her marbles.

Sofeet: Mem Sofeet is part of this family. It comes at the end of a word, sits on the line, and is always closed. Lucky for Mort, he gets to keep his marbles.

Sound: Molly, Mort and their marbles! Mem, Mem Sofeet "m" sound.

LAMED

Sarah:

OH NO!!! Lightning! I hate lightning.

Lily:

Rachel doesn't like lightning either. It's a little scary for her. But wow, that lightning looks a lot like the letter Lamed.

What makes Lamed special?

Shape: Lamed is long like lightning and lands on the line.

Sound: Lamed is like lightning. Lamed "l" sound.

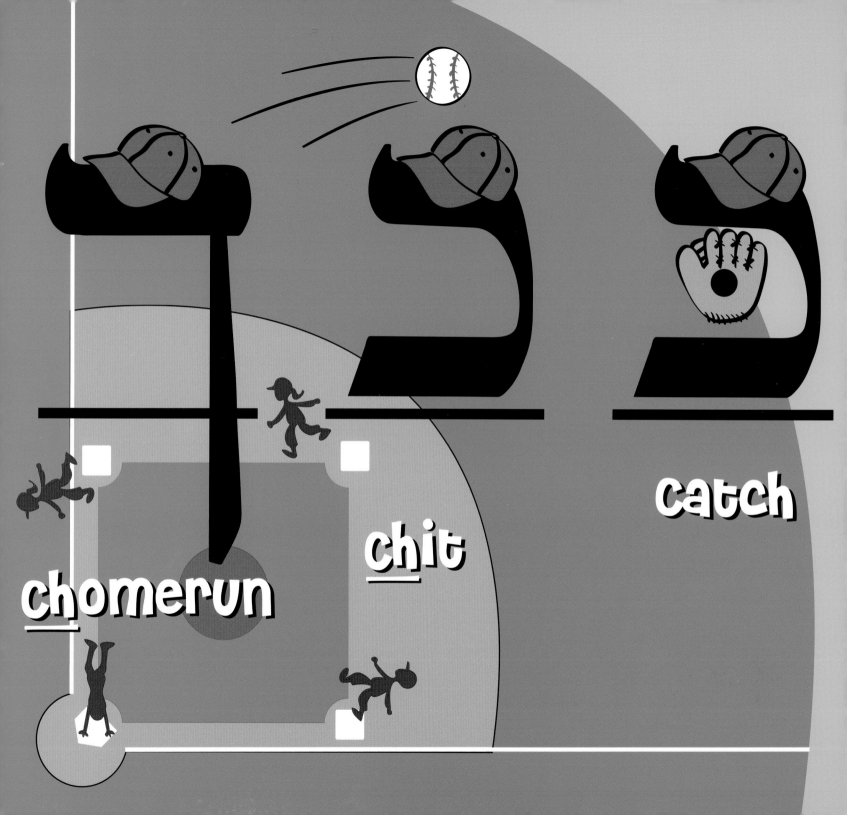

CAF CHAF CHAF SOFEET

David: Take me out to the ball game… wait a second, this is a weird ball game.

Lily: Well, maybe a little weird, but look at "Caf" catch! Look at "Chaf" chit, and "Chaf Sofeet" had a chomerun!! Caf, Chaf, Chaf Sofeet are on the same team, and they're a family!

What makes the Caf family special?

כ ב ך

Shape: Caf and Chaf are all curves and open on the left. Caf has a dot in the middle, but Chaf does not.

Sofeet Letters: Chaf Sofeet is a final letter, and like feet,  sofeet letters are always at the end of a word. Chaf Sofeet extends below the line.

Sound: Caf makes a "k" sound. The Chaf and Chaf Sofeet make that clear your throat "ch" sound.

So back to baseball… catch, chit, chomerun! Caf, Chaf, Chaf Sofeet "k, ch, ch" sound.

YUD

David:

Wow! Ben is floating around in outer space.

Lily:

What an adventure for Ben! Lucky for him he has the Yud to keep him company.
You see, Yud also floats in space! Yud is little, and it floats above the line.
In Hebrew words, the letters beside the yud keep it from floating
a-w-a-y………………………………

What makes Yud special?

Shape: Yud is a little curved letter that floats above the line.

Sound: Yud "y" sound.

TET

Sarah:

Why is there popcorn coming out of that letter Tet?

Lily:

Because Tet is open on top, and Tet can't hold all the popcorn inside.

What makes Tet special?

Shape: Tet is the only letter that's open on top. It sits on the line, and it's square on the bottom.

Sound: Tet. Top. Open. Tet "t" sound.

CHET

David:

What could Sarah possibly be dreaming about now? She's too young to get married.

Lily:

A girl is never too young to dream about her wedding day. That's Sarah under the chuppah with her prince charming!

David:

A chew-pah?

Lily:

No, a choo-pah. At their wedding, Jews stand under a choo-pah. The choo-pah represents the home that the couple will build together. And the letter Chet looks just like that choo-pah.

What makes Chet special?

Shape: Chet has two legs that sit on the line. And both legs are connected to its top.

Sound: Chet is also special because it makes the "chhhh" sound, the sound you make when clearing your throat. In Hebrew, there's no "ch" sound like in chair, so clear your throat and say "chhhh."

Chet looks like a choo-pah. Chet "ch" sound.

ZYIN

David:

Looks like Ben is zooming over the top of that letter. What is it?

Lily:

Ben is zooming over the Zyin.

What makes Zyin special?

Shape: Zyin is special because it has one leg that sits on the line and a curvy top.

Sound: Ben zooms over the zig-zagging Zyin. Zyin "z" sound.

vah vah vay veh vee voo vih

vo voo

VAV

Sarah:

Look at David! He's on Broadway!

Lily:

Yes that's David and the Fantastic Violet Vavs!

What makes Vav special?

Shape: Vav has one leg that sits on the line. The top is short and round.

Sound: Did you know that the Fantastic Violet Vavs sing and dance? If you look closely, you'll notice that each of the Vavs has a vowel underneath it. In Hebrew, the vowels are symbols that come below, beside, or above the letters. Can you guess what the different vowel sounds are? Let's try them together:

| AH | AH | AY | EH | EE | OO | IH | OH | OO |

Now, clap your hands and catch the beat of the Fantastic Violet Vavs!

Vah-Vah   Vay-Veh   Vee-Voo   Vih-Voh   Voo

David loves the Fantastic Violet Vavs. Vav "v" sound.

6

HEY

David:

Why does Rachel look sad? Is Hey in the hospital?

Lily:

Rachel is sad because Hey is hurt. Hey has a broken leg! You would be sad too.

What makes Hey special?

Shape: You see, Hey has two legs that sit on the line, but the left leg is broken! It doesn't connect to the top of the letter.

Sound: Hey hurts "h" sound.

DALED

Sarah:

Why is David pointing to a cobweb?

Lily:

He's a little grossed out. Daled has this dusty, dark, dirty, dented corner that **CREEPY** things love.

What makes Daled special?

ד

Shape: Daled has one leg that sits on the line and has that dusty, dark corner that makes it spooky and special.

Sound: Daled has a dusty, dark corner. Daled "d" sound.

4

GIMEL

David:

Why is Sarah dreaming about… shoes?

Lily:

Not just any shoes… high-heel shoes! I bet you're wondering what high-heel shoes could possibly have to do with the letter Gimel. Well, let's say that Gimel looks like a high-heel shoe.

What makes Gimel special?

Shape: Gimel sits on the line but has a gap that makes it look like a high-heel shoe!

Sound: Sarah can't wait to wear high-heel shoes!

Gimel has a gap. Gimel "g" sound.

VOOP   Benny

BET VET

David:

Benny and Voop? That's like Bet and Vet!

Lily:

Exactly. Bet and Vet are a pair, a family like Benny and Voop. Why are they a family?
Well, Bet and Vet look a lot alike.

What makes Bet and Vet special?

Shape: Bet and Vet sit on the line. They both have a little tail extending from the bottom right corner and are open on the left side. But be careful. They are also different. Bet has a belly button.

Sound: That belly button gives Bet the "b" sound. Vet has no belly button. It makes the "v" sound.

Benny and Voop are very best buddies. Bet "b" sound. Vet "v" sound.

ALEPH

Sarah:

Looks like Rachel likes to sing… AHHHHHHHH.

Lily:

Yes she does. And right now, she's singing the letter Aleph!

What makes Aleph special?

Shape: It's the first letter of the Aleph Bet. It sits on the line. It has an arm on the right and a leg on the left.

Sound: Aleph makes the "ah" sound when the "ah" vowel is below it. In Hebrew, the "ah" vowel looks like T or ▬ . More about vowels later.

Let's sing along with Rachel, "ahhhhhhhhh." Aleph "ah" sound.

Welcome to the Aleph Bet Story and the Hebrew alphabet!
Each letter tells a story!

Sarah and David, and their friends Ben, Rachel and *Lily*, can't wait to tell you their story too. Sarah's a bit of a dreamer. David's quite the performer. Ben finds himself in all sorts of situations. And Rachel likes to sing.

You'll meet them all inside.

Each letter in the Aleph Bet is special.
What should you look for?

* ✳ Corners or curves
* ✳ Openings or closings
* ✳ Letters on the line or dropping below it
* ✳ Dots
* ✳ Arms, legs, toes or tails

And now, Sarah and David bring you the Aleph Bet!

Sarah   David

The Aleph Bet Story

by
Lily Yacobi and Diana Yacobi

pictures by
Sari Bourne

Sarah and David Publications   Englewood, New Jersey

Pictures by Sari Bourne
Interior Design by Janet Jackson

ATTENTION SYNAGOGUES AND OTHER PROFESSIONAL OR EDUCATIONAL ORGANIZATIONS: Quantity discounts are available on bulk purchases of this book for educational and gift purposes. For information, please contact Sarah and David LLC, PO Box 5894, Englewood, NJ 07631 or info@sarahdavid.com.

The
Aleph Bet
Story